KT-483-669

I have this little
sister Lola.
She is small
and very funny.

Now Mum and Dad
say she is nearly
quite big enough
to go to school.

Lola is not
so sure.

lauren child

I am TOO absolutely small for school

featuring **Charlie** and **Lola**

ORCHARD BOOKS

for Sofie and her
invisible friend
Søren Lorensen

and for Maisie, Clemmie,

Molly and Ella

Thank you to Goldy for taking all the photographs so beautifully

Thank you to Simon for his utterly routine and illustration, invaluable comments work has been asserted by her in for this

ORCHARD BOOKS, 96 Leonard Street, London EC2A 4XD, Orchard Books Australia, 32/45-51 Huntley Street, Alexandria, NSW 2015. ISBN 1 84121 554 3 (hardback) ISBN 1 84362 266 8 (paperback). First published in Great Britain in 2003, First paperback publication in 2004, Text and illustrations © Lauren Child 2003, The right of Lauren Child to be identified as the author and illustrator of this work has been asserted by her in accordance with the Copyright, Designs and Patents Act, 1988. A CIP catalogue record for this book is available from the British Library. Printed in Singapore 10 8 6 4 2 1 3 5 7 9

She says, "I probably do not have time to go to school. I am too extremely busy doing important things at home."

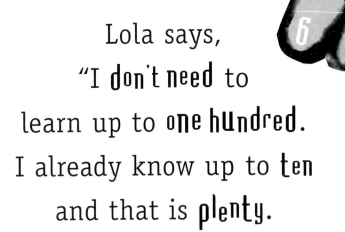

I say,
"At school
you will learn
numbers and how to
count up to one hundred."

Lola says,
"I don't need to
learn up to one hundred.
I already know up to ten
and that is plenty.

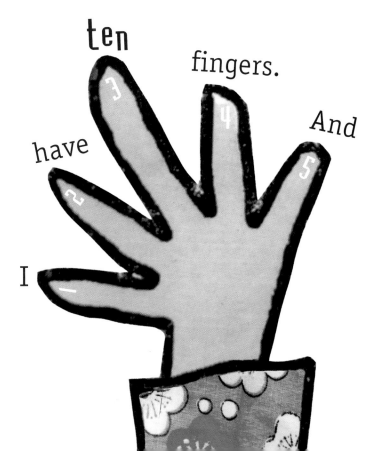

I have ten fingers. And

also I have ten toes.

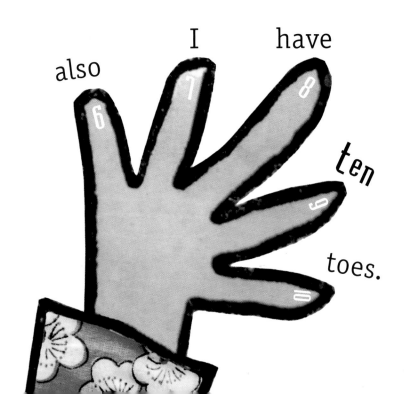

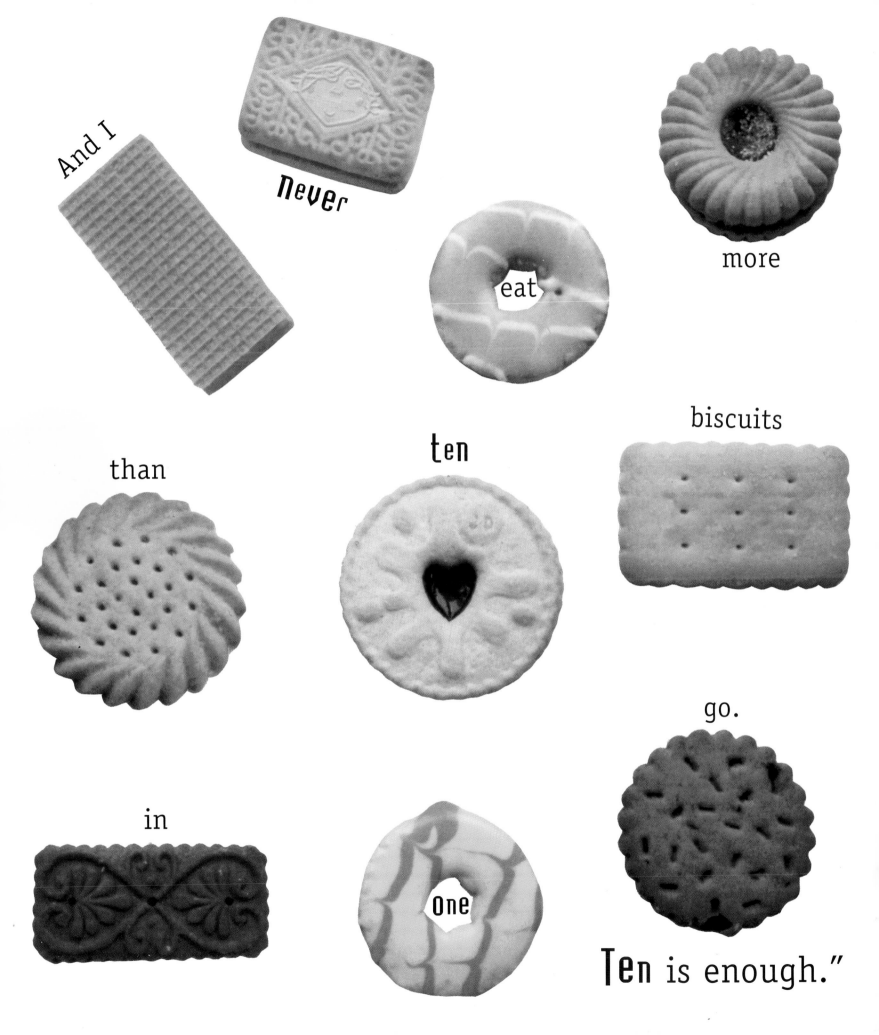

And I

never

more

eat

than

ten

biscuits

go.

in

one

Ten is enough."

"But Lola," I say, "what if eleven eager elephants all wanted a treat.

How would you count up how many treats that would be?

"Well," says Lola.

"I am not quite sure."

I say,

"And what about learning your

letters, Lola?

If you know how to write,

you can send cards to

people you like."

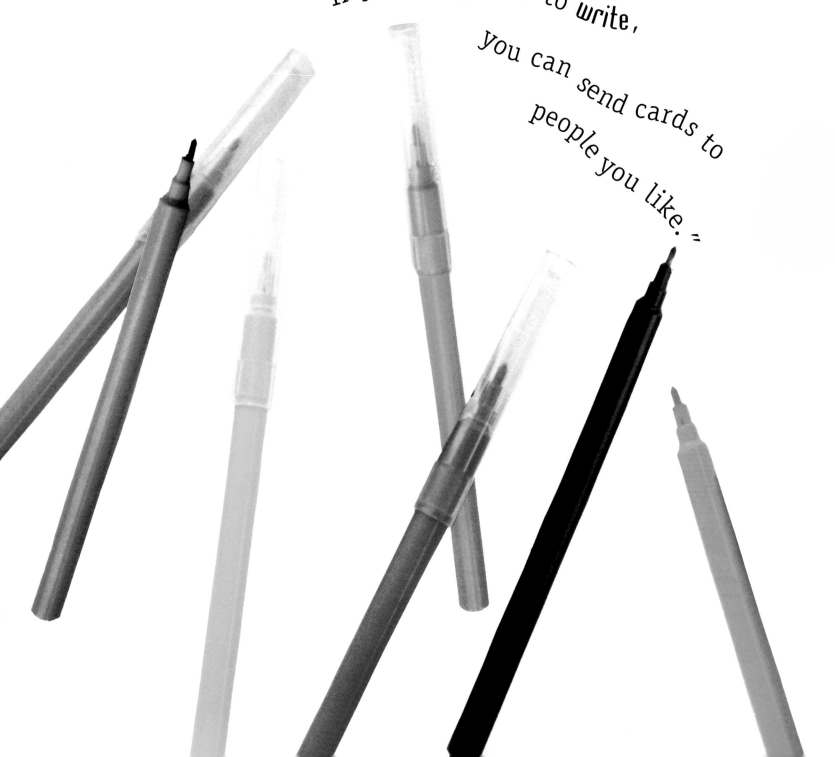

"But not everyone has a telephone you know," Lola, " I say.

"Who doesn't?" says Lola.

"Father Christmas," I say. "You have to write him a special note and put it up the chimney to tell

his little helpers your Christmas wish. Otherwise the little helpers might get your wish muddled up."

"I didn't know that, Charlie," says Lola.

"And Lola," I say,
    "don't you want to
read words? Then you will
        be able to **read** your
own **books**. And understand
secret messages written
on the fridge."

Lola says,
        "I know lots of **secrets**.
I don't need to **read words**,
            and I've got all my
books in my head.
            If I can't remember, I
can just make them up."

there is
pink milk
in this
fridge

"But Lola," I say, "what would you do if there was an ever so angry ogre who would not go to sleep unless you read him his favourite bedtime story?"

"I don't know, Charlie,"

says Lola.

Then Lola says,
"I **would** like to
read to an ogre and
count up elephants and
put **notes** up the chimbley.
But I **absolutely** will NOT
ever wear a **schooliform**.
I do not like wearing the
same as other people."

I say,
"But Lola, you do
not have to wear a
school uniform. At our
school you can wear
whatever you like."

"**Oh**," says Lola.
"You wait there. I know
exactly what I can wear..."

"Well, Lola," I say, "that certainly suits you,

but you **cannot** go to school dressed as a **crocodile**."

Lola says, "This is **not** a **crocodile**, this is a **alligator**."

I say, "You can't really go as an **alligator** either."

"Why not?" says Lola.

Charlie

"I like to wear stripes," says Lola, "but what will I do at lunchtime? You know I will NOT ever never eat a school dinner."

My sister Lola is fussy about food.

I say,
"But Lola, you can take your very own packed lunch in your very own lunch box."

Lola says, "I do not want to eat at school, **alone**, all by myself on my own."

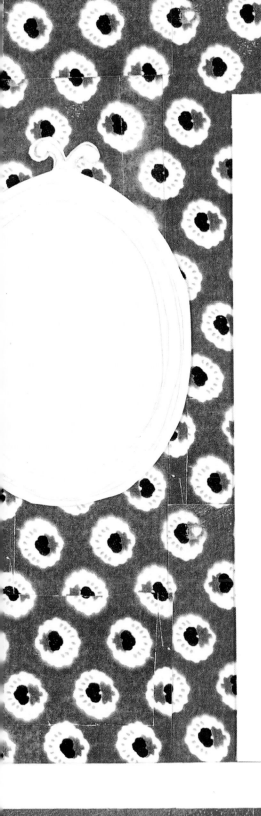

I say, "But Lola, at school you will meet lots of new **friends**. You can have **lunch** with one of them."

Then Lola says, "But I already have **my friend** Soren Lorensen. I would like to have **lunch** at **home** with him."

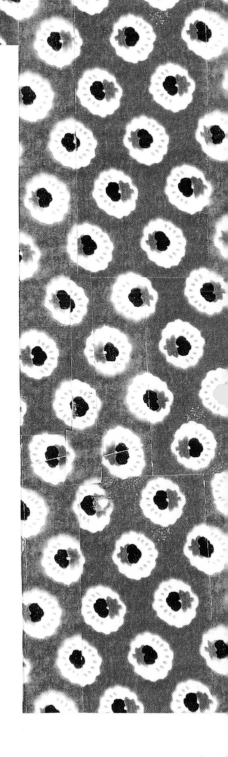

Soren Lorensen is Lola's invisible friend. No one knows what he looks like.

Walking to school, Lola is all wobbly.

She says, "Soren Lorensen is feeling slightly not very well.

He is worried he will not be able to count numbers, do letters and read words, and no one will

"Lola," I say, "it will be OK.

You'll be fine.

I bet you'll both have a really good time.

And after school we'll have pink milk at home."

"Lola," I say, "it will be OK.

talk to him so he will be all by himself on his own."

But all day I am **worried.**

I don't see her at break,

and she's nowhere at lunch.

I can't find her at hometime, she's not by her peg.

But then there she is, and she's not all alone by herself, she's hopping along home with somebody else...

At home, I say,
"Lola, I **told you** that you would have a **good time**."
And Lola says,
"Oh I know Charlie, I was not worried. It was Soren Lorensen who was nervous, **not me**. I was **fine**."